Do you still love me?

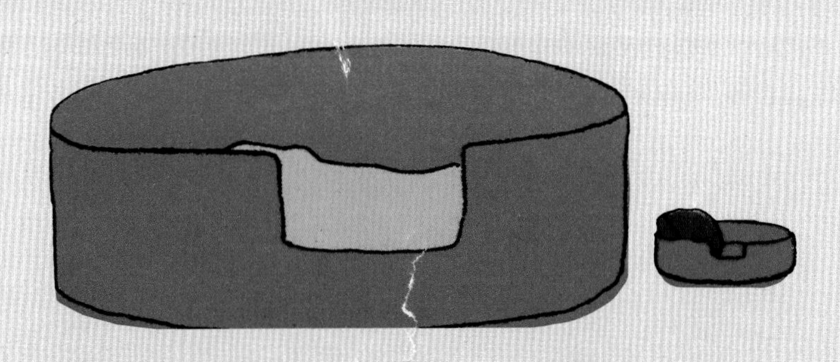

Albury Books

For Grandma

- Charlotte

First published in 2002 by Gullane Children's Books
This edition published in 2018 by Albury Books
Albbury Court, Albury, Thame, Oxfordshire, OX9 2LP

www.AlburyBooks.com

A CIP Record of this title is available from the British Library.

ISBN: 978-1-910571-49-1

Printed in Turkey.

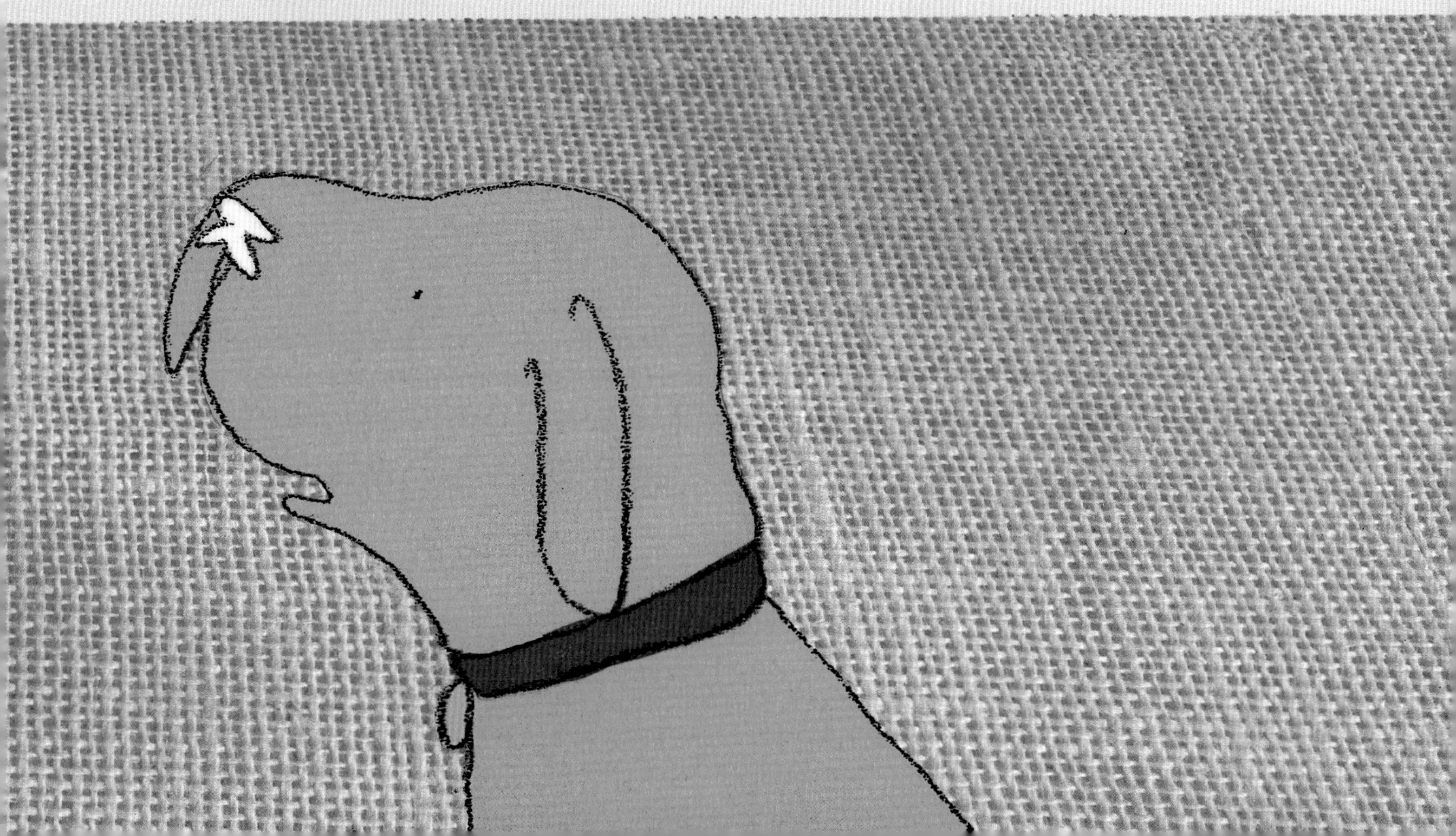

Every day,
Dudley liked to wake up early.

And every day,
he ate a hearty
breakfast.

Dudley's favourite game was hide-and-seek.

He liked to impress Aunt Pym with his fleas.

BARK!

But most of all,

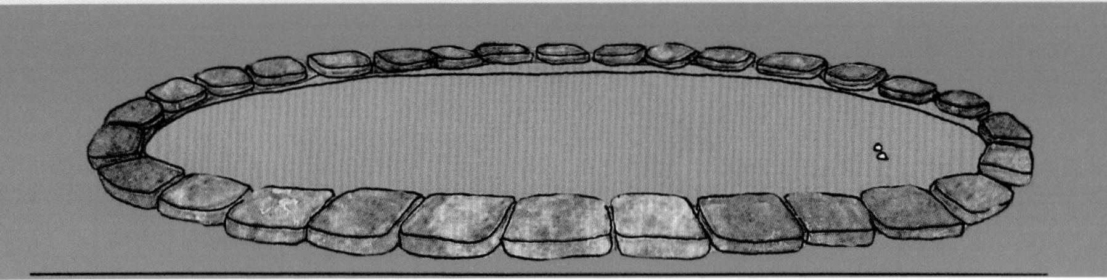

Dudley liked scaring Gemma,

the neighbour's cat.

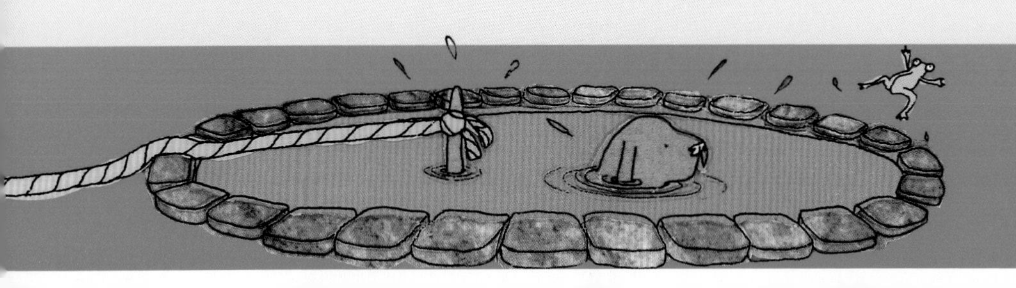

CHAMELEONS
What's so special about chameleleons?
Chameleons belong to the lizard family and have many unusual characteristics.
Their two eyes can move in different directions at the same time, which allows them to see all the way round their heads! A lot of chameleons can also change color!

Every evening,
Dudley curled up with Anna
in their favourite place.

Then one day Anna brought home someone new. It was a baby chameleon, called Pequito. From then on, things weren't the same.

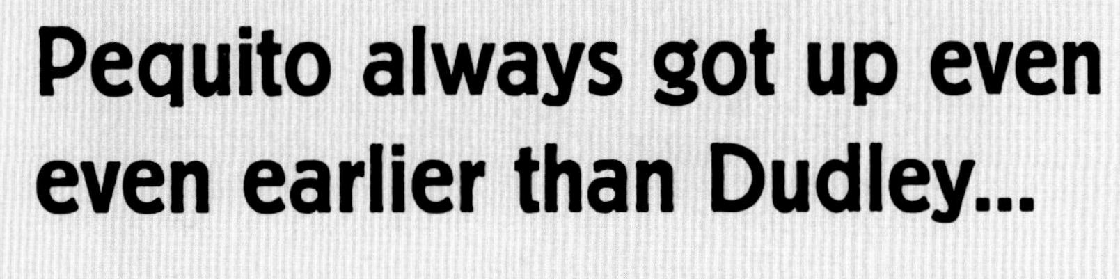

Pequito always got up even
even earlier than Dudley...

So Anna
was already up.

Pequito could
catch his own
breakfast.

Pequito was better at hide-and-seek.

Pequito was better at impressing Aunt Prym although he didn't have fleas.

All of Anna's friends were facinated by Pequito's funny eyes.

And no one noticed Dudley.

Chameleons have very long tongues (sometimes longer than their bodies). They use their tongues to catch insects to eat.
They usually live in warm places like deserts and rainforrests.
Some make their homes on the ground; some live in trees or bushes. They are very good climbers.

**And at the end of the day,
there was someone else
in Dudley's favourite place.**

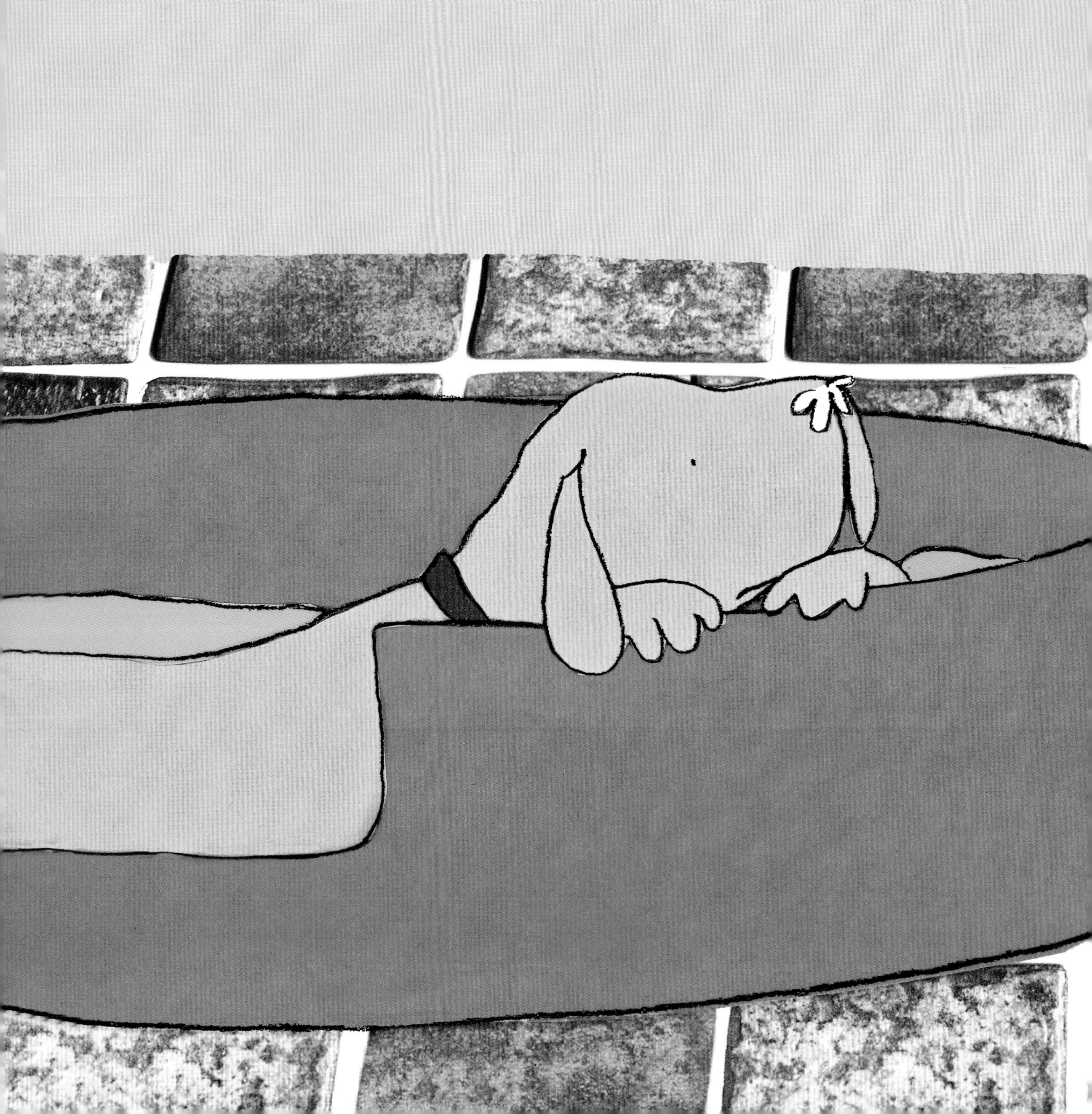

Dudley felt really sad.
Pequito was better at everything and
nobody seemed to care about Dudley any more.

Later on,
when Dudley woke up,
Pequito was gone.

Dudley was glad.

But when Pequito
didn't come back,

Dudley began to
get worried.

Dudley thought he had better look for him . . .

But somebody else
had already found Pequito.

Dudley barked louder
than he had every barked before.

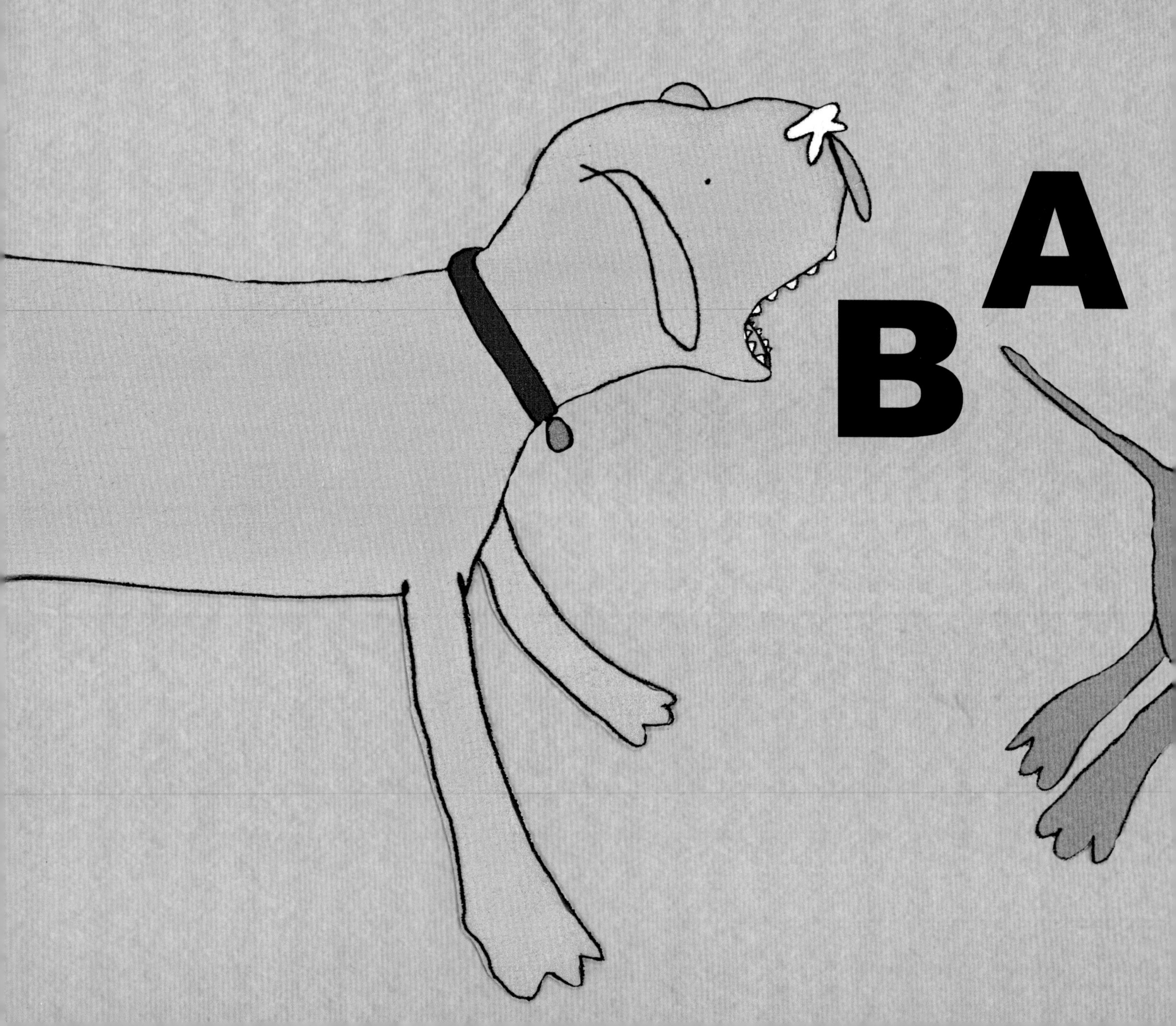

R K !

Anna and Pequito thought Dudley was a **hero!**

Giraffes
Are the tallest animals on land, between 4 and 5m tall. Their necks are over 2m long and used for reaching up to eat leaves from trees.
Giraffes are found only in Africa, on savannahs and grassland.
They mostly live in groups.
Every giraffe's coat has a unique pattern of brown spots or patches. Giraffes almost always sleep standing up.

From then on,
Dudley spent a lot of time
doing something he was REALLY good at . . .

Looking after Pequito.